Ten.

2.

Bo
a

# Pirate Adventures

Russell Punter

Illustrated by Christyan Fox

Reading Consultant: Alison Kelly
Roehampton University

# Contents

## Chapter 1

# The return of Captain Spike

On the edge of Rotters' Isle stood a prison for pirates. No one had ever escaped from the fortress's doomy dungeons.

The most famous prisoner was wicked Captain Spike. He was so mean, even the other pirates hated him.

Sneaky Spike just couldn't stop stealing. From the day he arrived, things went missing...

4

On Monday,
Cut-throat Craig's
pocket watch
disappeared...

on Tuesday, Roger
Redbeard's silver
earrings vanished
in the night...

and on Friday,
Sidney Skull
couldn't find his
gold locket.

No one knew who the thief was. But Spike's cell mate, Bobby Bones, noticed the Captain's bag getting fuller.

When Spike wasn't creeping around, he was showing off to the other prisoners.

"No jail can hold me," he boomed. "I'll be out of this smelly rat hole within a month."

Bobby Bones had had enough of the loud-mouthed Spike.

"I bet you'll be back in prison in twenty-four hours," he jeered.

"Oh yes?" growled the
Captain. "What do you bet?"
"This!" cried Bobby, holding
up a crumpled piece of paper.

"If you stay out for more
than a day, I'll send you my
treasure map," Bobby offered.
Spike's one piggy eye
sparkled with greed.

"Address it to the Spyglass Inn," said Spike, with a grin. "It'll reach me there."

"If you fail," said Bobby, "I get everything in your bag."
Spike stroked his bushy beard thoughtfully. "You're on!"

That night, while his cell mate was asleep, Spike stole the map from under Bobby's pillow. Then he quietly unlocked the cell door with a fat, brass key.

Ha ha! So long matey.

"I'll bet the jailer hasn't even noticed this is missing," Spike chuckled to himself.

Sneaking past the guards, Spike crept out of the prison and down to the dock. Minutes later, he was sailing out to sea in a stolen boat.

Spike couldn't wait to find Bobby's treasure. The map had directions to Spoof Island. Using the stars to guide him, he sailed through the night.

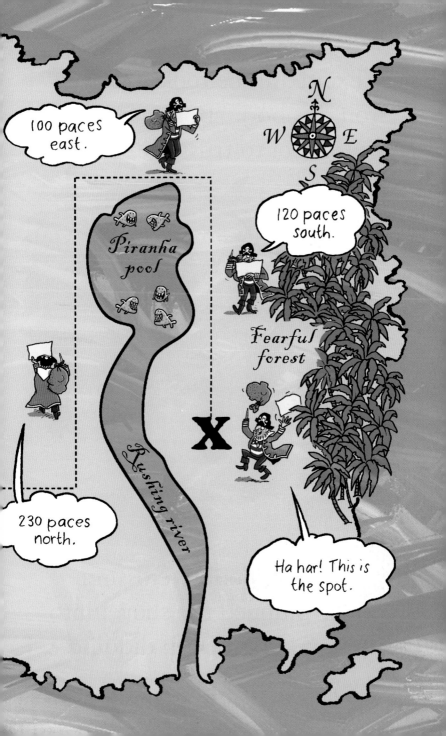

Excitedly, he took a shovel from his bag. "Bobby Bones was a fool to trust me," he growled.

Then the double-crossing pirate plunged the shovel into the sand and began digging...

deeper...

and deeper...

and deeper.

Spike felt the sand move
beneath him. "This is it!" he
gasped. With a final thrust, he
slammed the shovel in.

15

Spike tumbled down in a
mass of rubble, landing with a
bump. As the dust settled, he
stared around in disbelief.

16

"Welcome back, cell mate!" shouted Bobby Bones.

Stupid Spike had fallen for Bobby's trick. He had sailed around Rotters' Isle and was back where he started.

## Chapter 2

# Pirate of the Year

The final of the Pirate of the
Year contest was about to
begin. Pirates from around the
world had gathered to watch.

Only two contestants were left – Captain Blackheart and Billy Booty. The winner would take home a chest full of treasure.

**Ye scoreboard**

Blackheart    Billy

**RULES**

1. Cheating is expected. ( Just don't get caught! )

2. Pirates <u>must</u> protect each other against danger.

They had four tasks – and the first was a race. Each pirate had to sail his ship around Skull Island and back.

19

An ear-splitting boom from a cannon started them off. The pirates raised their anchors and the ships left port.

Billy and his crew took an early lead. By the time the ships were out of sight of the judges, they were way ahead.

But sneaky Blackheart had a trick up his ragged sleeve. "Alright lads," he barked. "Out with the secret weapons!"

Flaps opened in his ship's hull and ten oars shot out. Blackheart's crew began rowing as fast as they could.

"That's cheating," yelled Billy, as Blackheart raced by. "Remember rule one, Booty Brain," laughed his rival.

As the judges came within view, Blackheart's men pulled in their oars. Moments later, they sailed back into port.

"I win!" cried Blackheart.

| Blackheart | Billy |
|------------|-------|
| 1 | 0 |

For the next task, each pirate had to dive down to the sea bed and bring up a silver chest.

Blackheart gave Billy a hug. "Good luck, matey," he said.

The pirates plunged into the water and dived to the depths.

Spotting a chest, Billy tucked it under his arm.

But as he headed back, he was surrounded by hungry sharks. In the struggle to escape, he dropped the chest.

Billy had to come up for air. Seconds later, Blackheart surfaced holding a chest.

"Bad luck, Shark Bait," he snorted.

| Blackheart | Billy |
|:----------:|:-----:|
| 2 | 0 |

As Billy trudged ashore, he felt something slimy in his pocket. It was a smelly sardine. "So that's why Blackheart hugged me," he thought.

He knew the sharks would come after this fish.

Parrot training was the third task. The pirate with the most talkative bird would win. Billy's parrot, Mimi, went first.

"Beat that, Blackheart," said Billy proudly.

"Ha!" scoffed his opponent. "Wait until you hear my bird Hook Beak."

Hook Beak was declared best bird. The judges hadn't realized one of Blackheart's crew was doing all the talking.

Blackheart poked Billy in the tummy. "You may as well go home now," he said, with a grin.

Blackheart   Billy
    3          0

Everyone sailed to Skull Island for the final task. Each pirate was given a map. The first to find their buried treasure chest would win.

Blackheart's Map

N

12 paces north
22 paces west
14 paces north
9 paces west

X

Start

Billy's Map

N

X

21 paces north
15 paces east
17 paces north
16 paces east

Start

Billy looked at his map. Something about it didn't seem right. But there was no time to hesitate.

The pirates paced out their routes. Blackheart was so slow at counting, Billy was soon ahead.

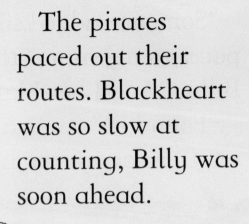

...fifteen, sixteen...

...seventee... OUCH!

But Billy's eyes were on the map – not where he was walking.

He marched straight into a rock pool full of angry crabs.

"Someone added six extra paces to my map," thought Billy. "And I bet I know who."

"Found it!" came a grizzly cry from across the island.

Blackheart had dug up his chest. He ran back to the start to show the judges. Suddenly he felt his legs being sucked down.

"Help!" he yelped. "I'm stuck in quicksand. I'm sinking fast."

Billy raced across the island. "Grab this!" he cried, snapping a branch from a palm tree.

As the gloopy sand dragged him down, Blackheart reached for the branch.

Billy used all his strength to pull his rival to safety.

The pirates who'd gathered
around gave a loud cheer.

"Well done, Billy," they cried.

"I still won the task," sneered
the ungrateful Blackheart.

"One point for
Blackheart," agreed
a judge. "But five bonus
points to Billy for
saving his life. So Billy
is Pirate of the Year!"

Blackheart Billy
4      5

## Chapter 3

# The cabin boy's secret

Harriet Hill helped her parents run a sheep farm by the sea. They were poor, but happy.

One day, a stern-looking man stomped up to the farmhouse.

"It's Sir Rollo Pinchly, the sea trader," Mr. Hill whispered to Harriet.

Pinchly flung a tiny bag of coins at Harriet's dad. "I want to buy this place," he bellowed.

"We love Curly Fleece Farm," said Mr. Hill. "We'll never sell."

Pinchly's face went scarlet. "No one refuses me," he roared, storming off. "I want this land for a new dockyard. And I'll get it somehow..."

The next day, disaster struck. The Hills woke to find that their sheep had vanished.

"We're ruined," sobbed Mrs. Hill. "Now we'll have to sell."

"I won't let Pinchly take our home," said Harriet. "I'll find a job in town and earn some money to buy more sheep."

Harriet packed some clothes and kissed her parents goodbye. But when she got to town, there were no jobs anywhere.

Harriet had almost given up, when she saw a sign by a ship in the docks.

Cabin boy
wanted – apply
The Salty
Seadog

"I need that job," thought Harriet. She hid behind some barrels and put on...

a pair of shorts...

a headscarf...

and a long, stripy shirt.

37

Minutes later, she was in the captain's cabin. "I want to be a cabin boy," she said gruffly.

"What's your name, lad?" asked Captain Cutlass.

"Um... Harry," replied Harriet, nervously.

"Hmm," said the captain, cautiously. "You're a bit skinny, but you're hired."

Once she was at sea, Harriet found life rather strange.

She and the other sailors were taught about...

 sword fighting...

lock blasting...

 and making people walk the plank.

She soon realized that *The Salty Seadog* was no ordinary boat – it was a pirate ship!

One morning, a cry came from a pirate high in the crow's nest.

SHIP AHOY!

"Her deck's full of cargo," added the lookout excitedly.

"Let's board her and grab it, lads!" cried Cutlass. "You stay and steer the ship, Harry."

Harriet watched the pirates go to work. They swung across to the other ship...

 chased its crew...

and tied them up.

But the pirates' luck was about to run out.

A heavy sail whooshed down from above and swamped them.

Harriet gasped when she saw who'd dropped the sail – Sir Rollo Pinchly. "Nobody steals from me," he snarled, as he untied his crew.

42

The pirates were locked in a cabin. "I'll have to rescue them," thought Harriet.

When Pinchly and his crew went below, Harriet swung across.

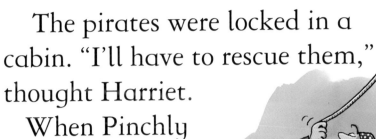

She slid back the bolt on the cabin door and freed her friends.

Well done Harry.

"Back to the *Seadog*, boys," hissed Cutlass.

Suddenly, Harriet heard a familiar noise coming from a crate. She peeked inside.

The noise alerted Pinchly and his crew. "Hands off my cargo!" he growled at Harriet.

"I recognize those curly coats," fumed Harriet, pulling off her headscarf. "Those are my dad's sheep."

Harriet told her story. Cutlass looked furious. At first, Harriet thought he was mad at her for pretending to be a boy.

But it was Pinchly who felt the pirate captain's rage.

"You scurvy scoundrel!" he boomed. "Even a pirate never steals from poor folk."

Pinchly's sailors knew nothing about the theft.

"Shame on you, Pinchly!" said one. "Give her sheep back!"

"Let's take him home for trial," shouted another.

"What about Cutlass and his crew?" asked a third.

"Don't take the pirates," begged Harriet. "After all, they did help find my sheep."

Pinchly's men agreed.

"Three cheers for Harry!" the pirates cried, and made her a lifelong member of *The Salty Seadog* crew.

Series editor: Lesley Sims

This edition first published in 2007 by Usborne Publishing Ltd.,
Usborne House, 83-85 Saffron Hill, London EC1N 8RT, England.
www.usborne.com
Copyright © 2007, 2006 Usborne Publishing Ltd.